The Yak Pack

Sight Word Comics

Book 4

Created by **r** rumack resources

Stories by Susan Muscovitch, M. Ed.
Illustrated by Jalisa Henry

Ruth Rumack's Learning Space
720 Spadina Ave., Suite 504
Toronto, Ontario, Canada M5S 2T9
www.ruthrumack.com
www.rumackresources.com

Book and Cover Design: Kathleen Fasciano and Jalisa Henry
Executive in Charge of Production: Evan Brooker
Managing Editor: Jennifer Makwana

ISBN: 978-0-9959587-7-7

PREFACE

What are sight words?

Sight words are the most common words that young readers come across. In 1948, Dr. Edward Dolch developed a list of the most frequently occurring words in books for children. He identified 220 words that make up 80% of what is written in typical children's books, and 50% of writing for adults. This became known as the "Dolch Word List". For this reason, sight words are also known as Dolch words, or high-frequency words. The entire Dolch Word List can be found at the back of this book.

Why learn sight words?

The 220 Dolch words are "service words" - they are pronouns, adjectives, adverbs, prepositions, conjunctions, and verbs. Most of the words do not follow decoding rules and cannot be sounded out. They have to be learned by "sight", or memorized. Even the words that are decodable should be recognized automatically, as they appear so frequently in stories. *The Yak Pack* series teaches sight words according to frequency, so the twenty words covered in each of the five books are among the 100 most common words your child will be exposed to when learning to read.

How do sight words help with reading?

Fluency in reading is essential to reading success. Once these basic sight words have been memorized and are instantly recognizable, emergent readers can read more fluently, and with greater comprehension. This frees up the cognitive energy to decode less frequent words, and allows children to focus on reading for meaning.

How to use this book:

• This book covers Dolch words 61-80, as sorted by frequency. Each story introduces two new words at a time, while reviewing previously learned words as well.
• Turn to the first story. Point to the two new words on the story title page and say them aloud, asking your child to repeat them.
• Review the previously learned words on the title page as well (if any).
• Read the story. Words that are not part of the sight word lists are depicted with images, and your child can attempt to read them with help from the pictures. (If your child cannot guess the word based on the image, tell the word to your child.)
• Once a full sentence has been read, have your child repeat it for increased fluency.
• After you read each story, complete the activities at the end for additional reinforcement.

Meet The Yak Pack!

ROD
THE FOX

ZAK
THE YAK

GUS
THE CUB

NICK
THE BUCK

TIFF & MEG
THE HARES

JACK
THE DUCK

PIP
THE PIG

JUD
THE PUP

ZIG, KIT, JIM & SID
THE KIDS

3

TABLE OF CONTENTS

STORY 31
I Am So Big!

New words introduced: big now

Review words: I / a / am / so / that / can / look
will / get / could / the / me

I was as little as a , but now I am so big!

bug

I am so big, that now I can  !

run

Look, I can  ___ now that I am big!

jump

I am so big now that I can .

swim

9

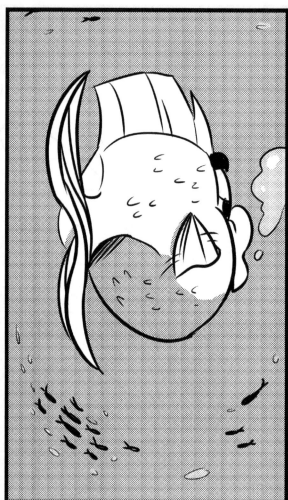

Now I will get a big !

fish

I am so big now that I could  a big 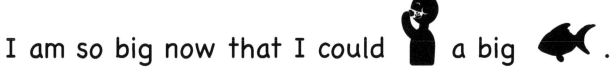 .

eat   fish

Now the big  will get me!

fish

After You Read: I Am So Big!

Trace the sight words, then try your own!

big   big   big   big   big

now   now   now   now   now

Additional Reinforcement:

1. Tape a piece of paper on the wall a little higher than your child's height. Ask your child to crouch down to the floor and say "I am little". Stretch up to the paper and write "Now I am big" on it.

2. Make a small word search using a 5x5 grid. Write the word "now" five times, either vertically or horizontally. Fill in the remaining boxes with more letters. Have your child search for and circle each "now".

STORY 32
The Long Walk

New words introduced: went long

Review words: we / to / look / at / a / the / had
so / in / down / for / and / then / out
was / of

We went to look at a long  .

log

 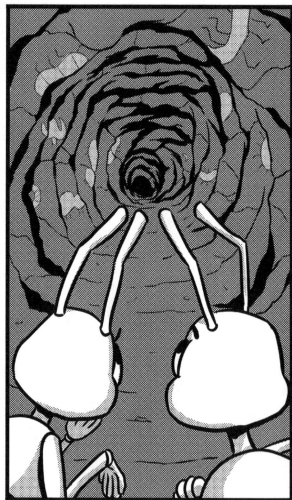

The long had a , so we went in.

log   hole

We went down a long  .

hole

The  was so long!

hole

We went for a long  down the long  .

walk   hole

19

We went down, down, and down...

And then we went out of the long

log

and we went to 🛏️ !

sleep

21

After You Read: The Long Walk

Trace the sight words, then try your own!

went went went went went

long long long long long

Additional Reinforcement:

1. Do a variety of different movements, like crawling, hopping, skipping, etc. Say, "I went for a long _____", spelling out "went" and "long" at the same time.

2. Draw a picture of a jungle, a city, and a beach. Write "I went for a long walk in the _____" underneath each drawing.

STORY 33
Eat Your Meat!

New words introduced: | are | no |

Review words: there / said / the / you / not / so / but
I / am / did / little / when / and / then
will / see

"There are no !" said the little .

bones wolf

You did not the , so there are no !

eat   meat   bones

But there are no  , so I am not  !

bones   happy

So the 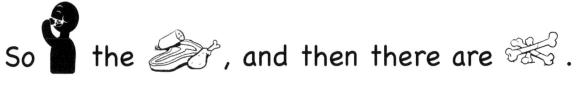, and then there are .

eat   meat   bones

No! I will not the if there are no !

eat   meat   bones.

There are 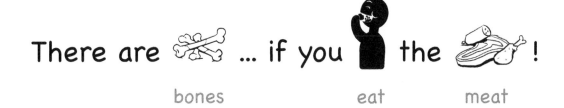 ... if you █ the █ !

bones   eat   meat

See! When you  the , there are !

eat   meat   bones

After You Read: Eat Your Meat!

Trace the sight words, then try your own!

are   are   are   are   are

no   no   no   no   no

Additional Reinforcement:

1. Draw a picture of an empty fridge or cupboard, and write 3 sentences about it, drawing pictures to fill in the blank. For example, "There are no drinks/potatoes/apples".

2. Do some actions together, such as clapping, jumping, stretching, etc. Say aloud what you are doing, spelling out the word "are". For example, "We A-R-E clapping."

STORY 34
Come to My House!

New words introduced: | if | | come |

Review words: you / to / my / I / will / be / we / yes
could / and / there

If you come to my  , I will be ![]

house   happy

If I come to the  , will we 🏃 ?

house   play

34

Yes, if you come, we will   !

play   ball

If I come there, could we 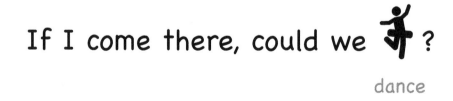?

dance

Yes, we will  if you come!

dance

Could we  if I come?

sing

Yes, if you come we will  and  and  !

sing   dance   play

After You Read: Come to My House!

Trace the sight words, then try your own!

if   if   if   if   if

come come come come come

Additional Reinforcement:

1. Plan an imaginary party, and make invitations that read: If you come, we will _____ . Fill in the blank with a picture of a party activity like eating cake or opening presents.

2. Paint "if" and "come"in watercolours.

STORY 35
The Lost Pig

New words introduced: ask came

Review words: him / if / he / with / his / I / will / no
not / did / and / said

Ask him if he came with his .

mom

I will ask him if he came with his .

dad

No! Ask if he came with 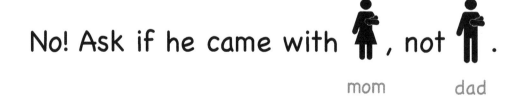, not 👤.

mom　　dad

I will ask him if he came with his .

bug

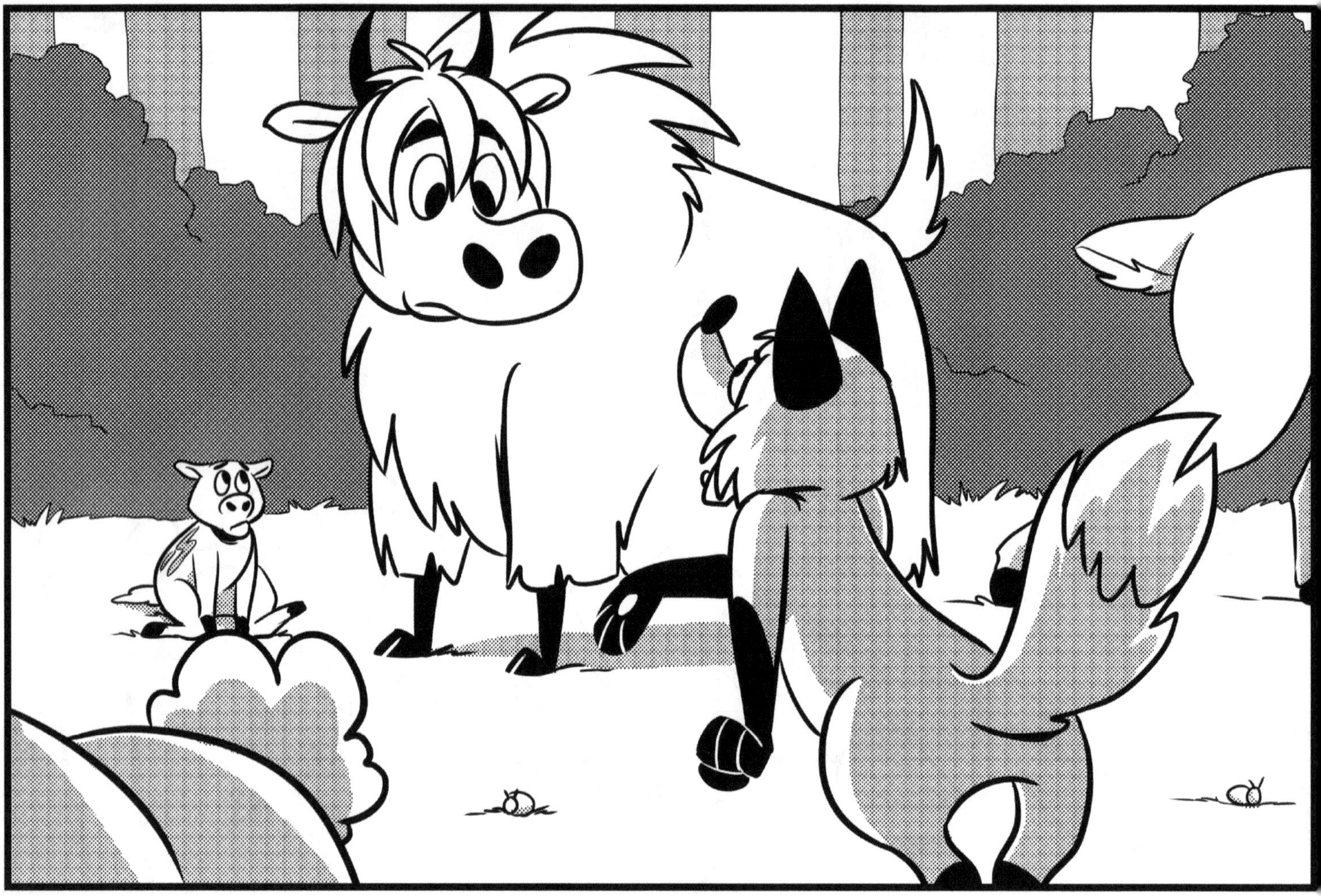

Not his 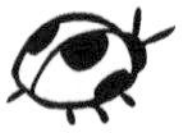 ! Ask if he came with his 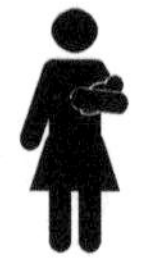 !

bug mom

I did ask if he came with his ...

mom

And he said he came with his and his !

bug   dad

48

After You Read: The Lost Pig

Trace the sight words, then try your own!

ask   ask   ask   ask   ask

came   came   came   came   came

Additional Reinforcement:

1. Write the letters for "ask" and "came" in random order, and have your child unscramble them and write them correctly.

2. Remember how to spell "came" with the mnemonic:

    <u>C</u>ats <u>A</u>nd <u>M</u>onkeys <u>E</u>verywhere

Draw a picture to help remember.

STORY 36
The Dark Cave

New words introduced: into ride

Review words: can / we / the / but / there / will / be
in / what / if / with / on / not / see / do

Can we ride into the  ?

cave

We can ride into the  ,

cave

but there will be in the  !

bats   cave

52

What if we ride into the  with on?

cave   hats

53

If we ride into the  with  on,

cave   hats

we will not see!

What if we ride into the  with  ?

cave   flashlights

If we ride into the  with ,

cave   flashlights

we will !

crash

What if we do not ride into the  !

cave

After You Read: The Dark Cave

Trace the sight words, then try your own!

into   into   into   into   into

ride   ride   ride   ride   ride

Additional Reinforcement:

1. Tell your child to imagine that he or she is a superhero and draw a superhero cave and vehicle. Write "I ride into the cave" underneath the picture.

2. Make the letters for "into" and "ride" out of playdough.

STORY 37
A Very Blue Day

New words introduced: $\boxed{\textsf{very}}$ $\boxed{\textsf{blue}}$

Review words: the / but / in / not / see / was / and
went / to / they / could / a / big

The  was very blue.

sky

60

The  and the went to the very blue .

yak   fox   lake

In the very blue  , they could

lake

see the very blue ⛰️ .

sky

They could see a very blue

bird

in the very blue .

sky

In the very blue  sky , they could see big  clouds .

They could see a big  in the very blue .

fish   lake

But the big  was not very blue.

fish

After You Read: A Very Blue Day

Trace the sight words, then try your own!

very very very very very

blue blue blue blue blue

Additional Reinforcement:

1. Color a sky from pale blue to vibrant blue. In each shade, write the word "blue". In the vibrant blue, write "very blue".

2. Find things around the house that are bright blue, and trace the words "very" and "blue" over them.

STORY 38
The Tail Monster

New words introduced: $\boxed{\text{just}}$ $\boxed{\text{your}}$

Review words: the / little / it / is / said / no / not
my / a / yes / now / do / see / then
big / up / to / his / he

The little ___ up to his .

wolf   jumps   mom

His 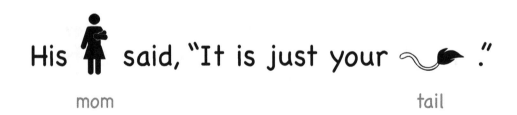 said, "It is just your 〰️🐭 ."

mom   tail

No, it is not just my  ... it is a 👹 !

tail   monster

Yes, it is just your little ! Now just do not 🏃.

tail   jump

72

Just my little ? See, it is a !

tail   monster

73

Your little  is just a , not a !

tail   tail   monster

The little 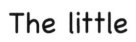 ___ ! Then he said,

wolf   jumps

"It is just your big  !"

tail

After You Read: The Tail Monster

Trace the sight words, then try your own!

just just just just just

your your your your your

Additional Reinforcement:

1. Take turns popping out of a hiding spot and shouting "Boo!" Then say "It was J-U-S-T Y-O-U-R mom/child/student etc."

2. Use this trick to remember how to spell "your":

   Do <u>YOU R</u>emember how to spell **YOUR**?

Write out the above sentence, with YOUR in a different color.

STORY 39
The Angry Ant

New words introduced: $\boxed{\text{over}}$ $\boxed{\text{an}}$

Review words: the / went / said / you / just / me
I / can / are / that / have / and

The  said, "Can you ___ over an 🐜 ?"

yak   jump   ant

The 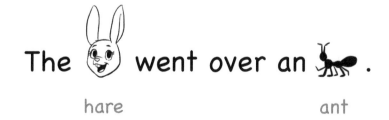 went over an 🐜.

hare　　　　　　　　　　ant

An  said, "You just went over me!"

angry   ant

The said, "Are you  that I went over you?

hare   sad

Have an ."

ice cream

81

The  said, "Can you ___ over an 🐏?"

yak   jump   ox

The 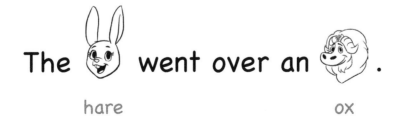 went over an .

hare   ox

An  said, "You just went over me!"

angry   ox

84

The said, "Are you that I went over you?
hare   sad

Have an ."
ice cream

An  and an ant have an ice cream

ox   ant   ice cream

and are  !

happy

After You Read: The Angry Ant

Trace the sight words, then try your own!

over ⋯over⋯ ⋯over⋯ ⋯over⋯ ⋯over⋯

an ⋯an⋯ ⋯an⋯ ⋯an⋯ ⋯an⋯

Additional Reinforcement:

1. Make 3 signs that read "jump", "over", and "an". Have your child print the signs for "over" and "an". Lay them in a row on the floor and place a picture or object that begins with a vowel at the end (e.g. an egg, an apple, etc.) Have your child read the sentence and then jump over the object.

2. Draw and cut out pictures of an apple, egg, insect, octopus, and umbrella. Using two cut-outs at a time, arrange one on top of the other and write "The _____ is over an _____". Repeat with other cut-outs to write as many sentences as desired.

STORY 40
The Fox with the Red Tail

New words introduced: its red

Review words: the / could / see / was / very / big
with / were / on / then / he / a / to

The 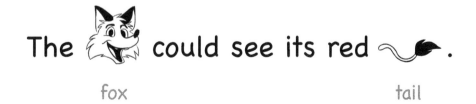 could see its red ~•.

fox   tail

Its red  was very big.

tail

The  its big red ～●.

fox   chased   tail

He could see a with red .

bird   feathers

Its red  were on its .

feathers   wings

93

The  to its red .

bird　　flies　　　　　　house

The  its red ,

fox   chased   tail

then  the red .

chased   bird

After You Read: The Fox with the Red Tail

Trace the sight words, then try your own!

its   its   its   its   its

red   red   red   red   red

Additional Reinforcement:

1. Draw a wild red creature, and label all of its parts. For example, its red head, its red feet, its red mouth, etc.

2. Ask "How do you know when a polar bear has a cold?" Have your child draw a picture of a polar bear with a cold and answer in writing: "Its nose is red."

CERTIFICATE OF ACHIEVEMENT!

This certificate is to show that:

_____

can read the sight words from List 4:

- big
- now
- went
- long
- are
- no
- if
- come
- ask
- came

- into
- ride
- very
- blue
- over
- an
- just
- your
- its
- red

Great Job!

Dolch Word Lists (by frequency)

LIST 1	
and	was
the	said
to	his
he	on
you	that
I	she
a	for
it	had
of	they
in	but

LIST 2	
is	out
with	go
at	as
there	little
look	we
up	have
him	am
her	down
all	then
some	be

LIST 3	
can	get
do	my
what	would
did	like
when	me
were	this
could	will
not	yes
see	them
so	one

LIST 4	
big	into
now	ride
went	very
long	blue
are	over
no	an
if	just
come	your
ask	its
came	red

Dolch Word Lists (by frequency)

LIST 5	
want	put
good	every
don't	too
know	pretty
how	jump
about	take
any	where
from	got
around	green
right	four

LIST 6	
saw	going
old	sleep
call	ran
away	help
here	let
by	make
think	five
their	yellow
after	six
well	brown

LIST 7	
two	never
walk	fly
play	stop
again	off
who	today
or	cold
been	myself
before	round
may	seven
eat	eight

LIST 8	
try	black
keep	white
tell	always
first	goes
must	write
give	ten
start	does
work	drink
much	bring
new	once

Dolch Word Lists (by frequency)

LIST 9	
soon	our
has	warm
made	better
find	buy
run	ate
only	full
gave	those
us	funny
open	hold
three	done

LIST 10	
out	sit
hurt	read
use	which
both	under
fast	fall
pull	why
say	carry
kind	own
pick	small
light	found

LIST 11	
wash	upon
hot	wish
live	many
clean	together
show	shall
draw	sing
because	thank
best	these
grow	please
far	laugh

About Rumack Resources

Rumack Resources is the publishing division of Ruth Rumack's Learning Space (RRLS), an educational support company specializing in early literacy. Since 1996, Ruth Rumack and her team have been providing individualized academic and special education support to students in Toronto, Canada. RRLS's approach to teaching through sensory and motor activities that are tailored to specific learning styles is evident in every Rumack Resources product. All products are developed and written by certified teachers with extensive experience in the early reading process.

Author Susan Muscovitch is a certified teacher at Ruth Rumack's Learning Space, with a Masters of Education and qualifications in special education. Susan lives in Toronto with her husband and daughter.

Titles available from Rumack Resources:

Phonological Awareness:	Phonics:	Sight Words:

Alpha-Mania Adventures	The Yak Pack: Comics & Phonics	The Yak Pack: Sight Word Comics
Storybooks that teach 5 phonological awareness skills: rhyming, blending, alliteration, segmenting, and sound manipulation.	Phonics readers in a fun, comic style! Book 1: Short Vowels Book 2: Digraphs Book 3: Blends Book 4: Bossy E	Stories to teach sight words! Book 1: Sight words 1-20 Book 2: Sight words 21-40 Book 3: Sight words 41-60 Book 4: Sight words 61-80 Book 5: Sight words 81-100

Printed in the USA
CPSIA information can be obtained
at www.ICGtesting.com
LVHW081237240823
756072LV00010B/731

9 780995 958777